Anna Obiols & Subi

Triceratops

The strongest dinosaur

BARRON'S

I have a friend.

He has three horns that

can be used as a coat rack.

He isn't a rhinoceros, although he looks a lot like one.

He can grow to weigh as much as an elephant.

He has a very pointed beak,

but he isn't a bird.

His jaws are like hedge clippers.

He is an excellent helper whenever the bushes

need trimming.

It's difficult to find a hat that fits him.

He likes living in a family. It's hardly surprising that, if you take him with you to the country and there is a herd of sheep, he starts grazing with them. It reminds him of the past.

I love climbing on his back and thinking

that I'm driving a four-wheel vehicle.

His body and legs are so strong that you can build a cabin on top of him with no fear of it falling down.

He likes kicking up a lot of dust to scare his enemies,

so I always have to walk behind him with a broom.

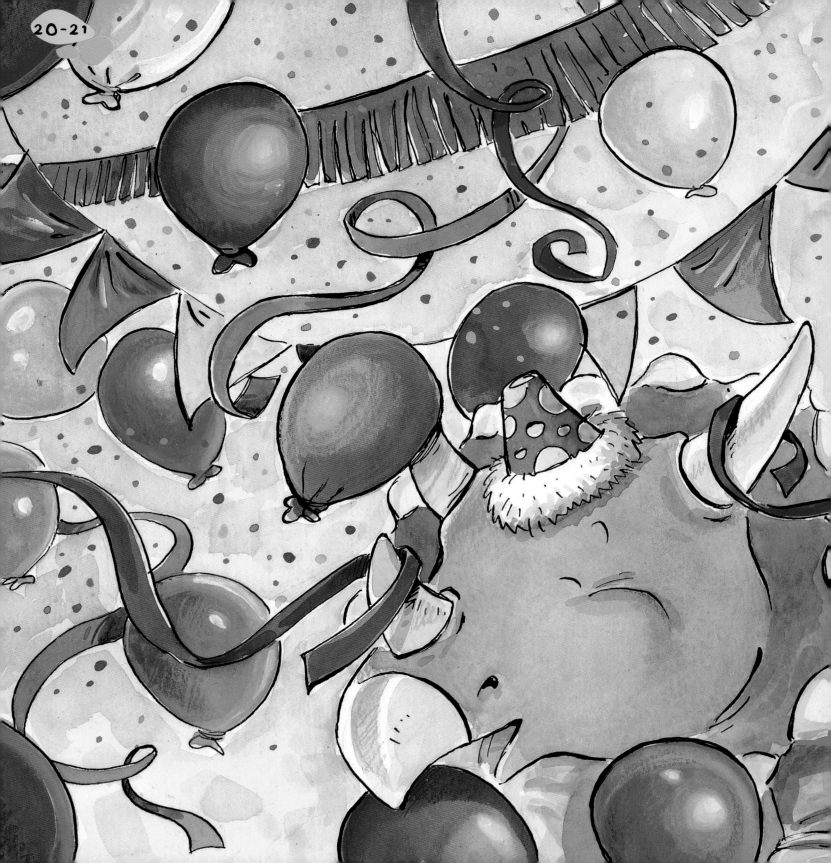

If you go to a birthday party and you end up playing to see who can pop the most balloons, my friend is the best teammate, because he can pop them all in an instant.

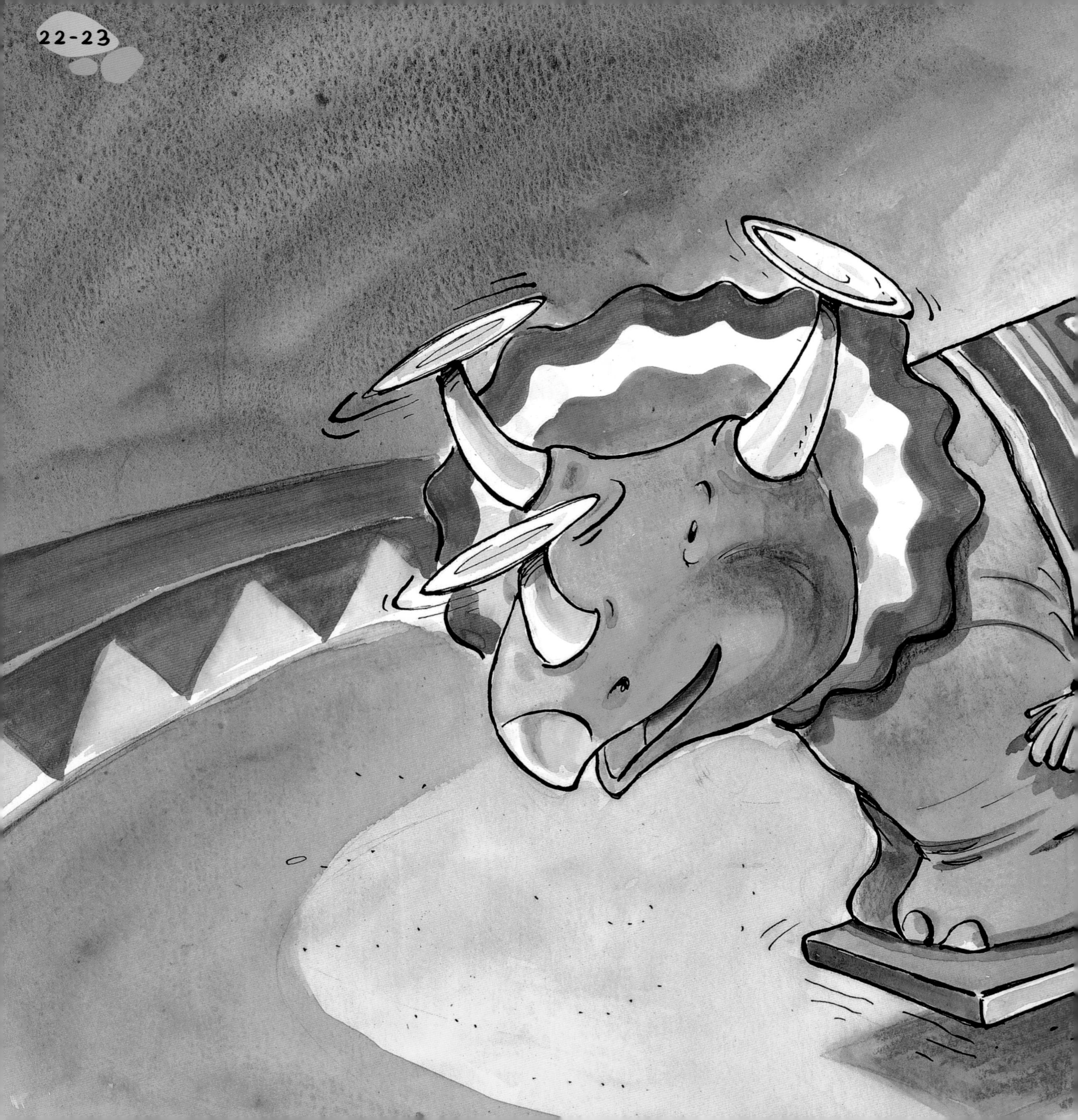

Sometimes we dream that

we are members of a circus.

And we spend a lot of time playing.

Do you know

who my friend is?

The TRICERATOPS

that sleeps with me every night.

Good night!

It had sunken eyes, thus protecting them easily.

It had front horns almost 3.3 feet (1 meter) long.

It had a third horn, short but powerful.

The Triceratops

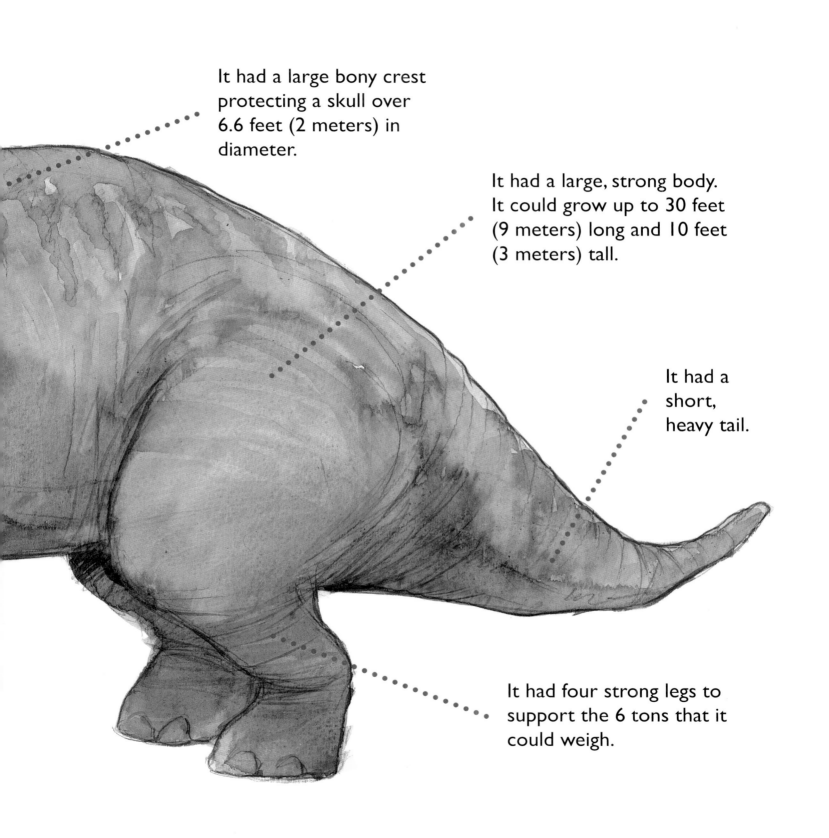

It had a large bony crest protecting a skull over 6.6 feet (2 meters) in diameter.

It had a large, strong body. It could grow up to 30 feet (9 meters) long and 10 feet (3 meters) tall.

It had a short, heavy tail.

It had four strong legs to support the 6 tons that it could weigh.

SCIENTIFIC DESCRIPTION OF THE TRICERATOPS

Its name means "three-horned face." It was one of the last dinosaurs to walk the Earth. It lived at the end of the Cretaceous period, and it lived during the same period as tyrannosaurus rex.

The Cretaceous covers the period from 135 to 65 million years ago. The two continents (north and south) present during the Jurassic period gradually changed to become the modern day continents. During this period, the climate was much colder, the seasons were very different, and the first flowers appeared.

FUN FACTS:

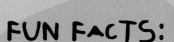

- Its neck bones were particularly strong, as were the hip and upper skull bones.
- It walked at a speed of 6 miles/hour (10 kilometers/hour); but over short distances, it could reach 15 miles/hour (25 kilometers/hour).
- Although it looks like a rhinoceros, it was twice as large and not a mammal, but a reptile.

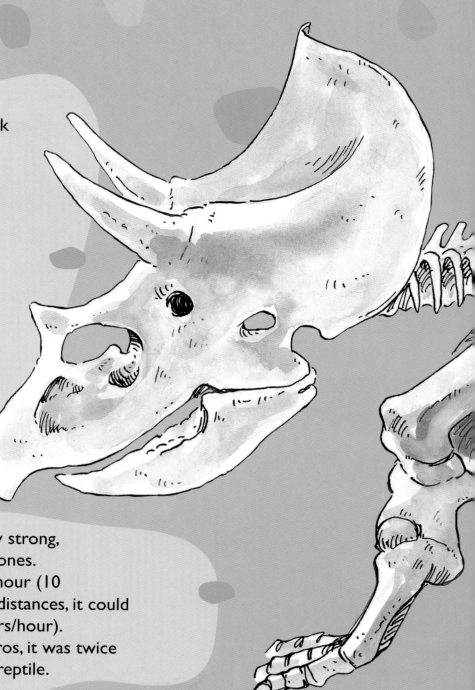

CHARACTERISTICS

Triceratops was a plant-eater with a pointed beak and sharp teeth so it could chew hard leaves and roots. Its beak wore down with use, but it continued to grow throughout the dinosaur's entire life, similar to the way our nails grow.

The triceratops was recognized above all for the horns on its forehead and neck. In addition to being used as weapons, it is thought that they were used to gain territory when faced with a rival or for mating. The triceratops also had a bony crest on its neck. This made its head look larger and much more threatening.

It was one of the strongest dinosaurs. This means that it was not an easy target, even for the fearsome tyrannosaurus rex.

It had great strength for facing enemies and, as a defensive strategy, it kicked up a cloud of dust to mix them up.

Triceratops lived in large herds, and moved through forests, banks along water, and around swamps. It ate trees, bushes, and ferns.

It lived in the western part of the North American continent. The remains of about 1,500 individuals have been found.

General information about Dinosaurs

Their name means "terrible, powerful lizard" or "big reptile." The dinosaurs were a highly varied group of animals that lived on the Earth millions of years ago. The era in which they lived is divided into three great periods: the Triassic, the Jurassic, and the Cretaceous. Everything we know about these creatures is thanks to fossils, which are the remains of plants and animals that lived many years ago and have turned into stone. Thanks to these fossil remains—such as bones, footprints, skins, and eggs—we know what the dinosaurs ate, how they moved around, and how they were born. Paleontologists are scientists who study fossils. When they find the remains of a dinosaur, the first thing they have to do is dig them up very carefully. Then, all the material is sent to the laboratory, to prevent it from being damaged. The fossils are often wrapped in plaster,

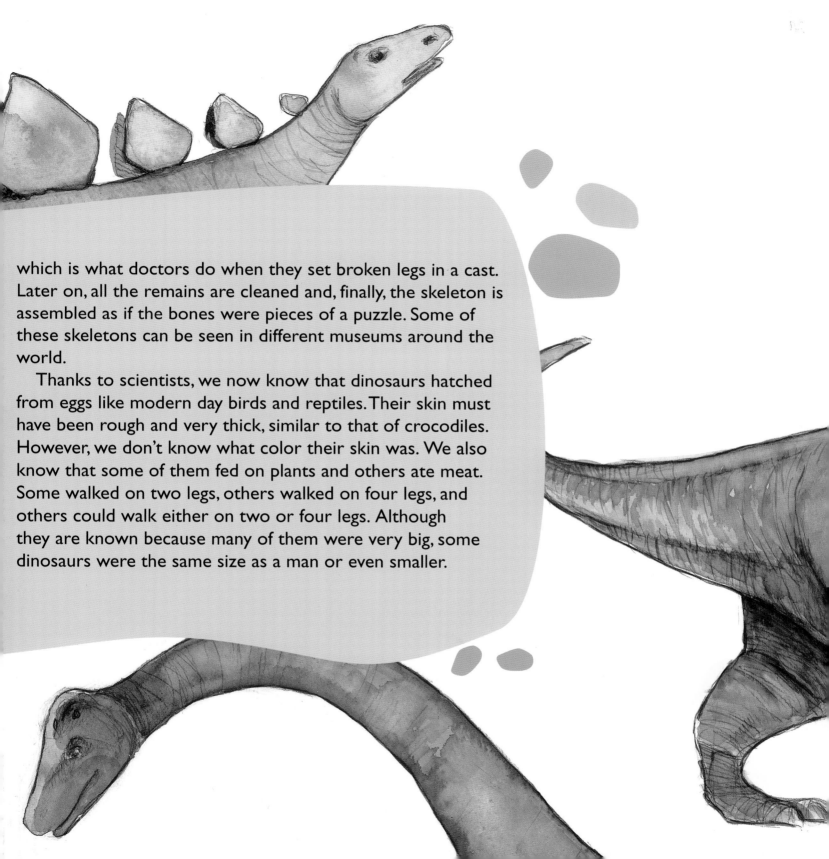

which is what doctors do when they set broken legs in a cast. Later on, all the remains are cleaned and, finally, the skeleton is assembled as if the bones were pieces of a puzzle. Some of these skeletons can be seen in different museums around the world.

Thanks to scientists, we now know that dinosaurs hatched from eggs like modern day birds and reptiles. Their skin must have been rough and very thick, similar to that of crocodiles. However, we don't know what color their skin was. We also know that some of them fed on plants and others ate meat. Some walked on two legs, others walked on four legs, and others could walk either on two or four legs. Although they are known because many of them were very big, some dinosaurs were the same size as a man or even smaller.

Triceratops

First edition for the United States and
Canada published in 2012 by Barron's
Educational Series, Inc.

© Copyright 2011 by Gemser Publications,
S. L., El Castell, 38, 08329 Teià, Barcelona, Spain

Author: Anna Obiols
Illustrator: Subi (Joan Subirana)
Design and layout: Gemser Publications, S. L.

All inquiries should be addressed to:
Barron's Educational Series, Inc.
250 Wireless Boulevard
Hauppauge, NY 11788
www.barronseduc.com

ISBN: 978-1-4380-0108-1
Library of Congress Catalog Number:
2011938895

Date of Manufacture: June 2012
Manufactured by: Discovery Printing Co. Ltd,
Dongguan, Guangdong, China

Printed in China
9 8 7 6 5 4 3 2 1